trilogy

&

Hagoromo:
A Celestial Robe

trilogy &

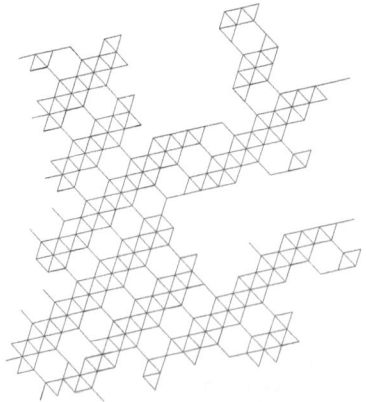

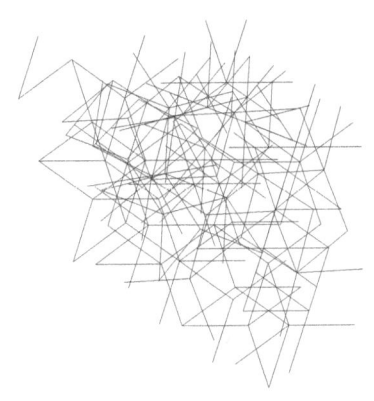

Hagoromo:
A Celestial Robe

Yoko Danno

The IKUTA PRESS

To Yoko
With love,
Anna Lewis Cu. 78

Table of Contents

trilogy

Foreword

"My lexicon was my only companion," wrote Emily Dickinson to the obtuse Higginson. Yoko Danno once wrote me, "I collect words from dictionaries until I come across a key word (or key words), then start choosing words again in the dictionaries to form a 'constellation' around the key word(s). I use English-English, Japanese-Japanese, English-Japanese, and Japanese-English dictionaries." Aside from this total absorption in words, there is no resemblance. Miss Dickinson's seclusion is known to all. Mrs. Iida is a young woman who lives in Kobe with her husband and their two children.

Her poetry is at once imagistic and abstract: imagist, because it consists almost entirely of images: abstract, because the coherence of the images is emotional, not discursive. The Imagist school of poets (by which of course we mean H. D.) avoided the abstract. "Go in fear of abstraction," warned their mentor, Ezra Pound. Nevertheless, in the same manifesto he called for "direct treatment of the 'thing' whether subjective or objective." H. D. gives us direct treatment of the object: a rose, a wave. Yoko Danno gives us direct treatment of the subject: herself. H. D.'s images relate to a definite topography. Her rose blooms in a real garden, her wave crashes on a real beach. Yoko Danno's images are autonomous. They are like Marianne Moore's real toads in imaginary gardens.

This poem, with its spiritual intensity and its impeccable craftsmanship, seems to me a perfect paradigm of Mallarmé's famous dictum, "Ce n'est point avec idées, mon cher Degas, que l'on fait des vers. C'est avec des mots."

Lindley Williams Hubbell (1970)

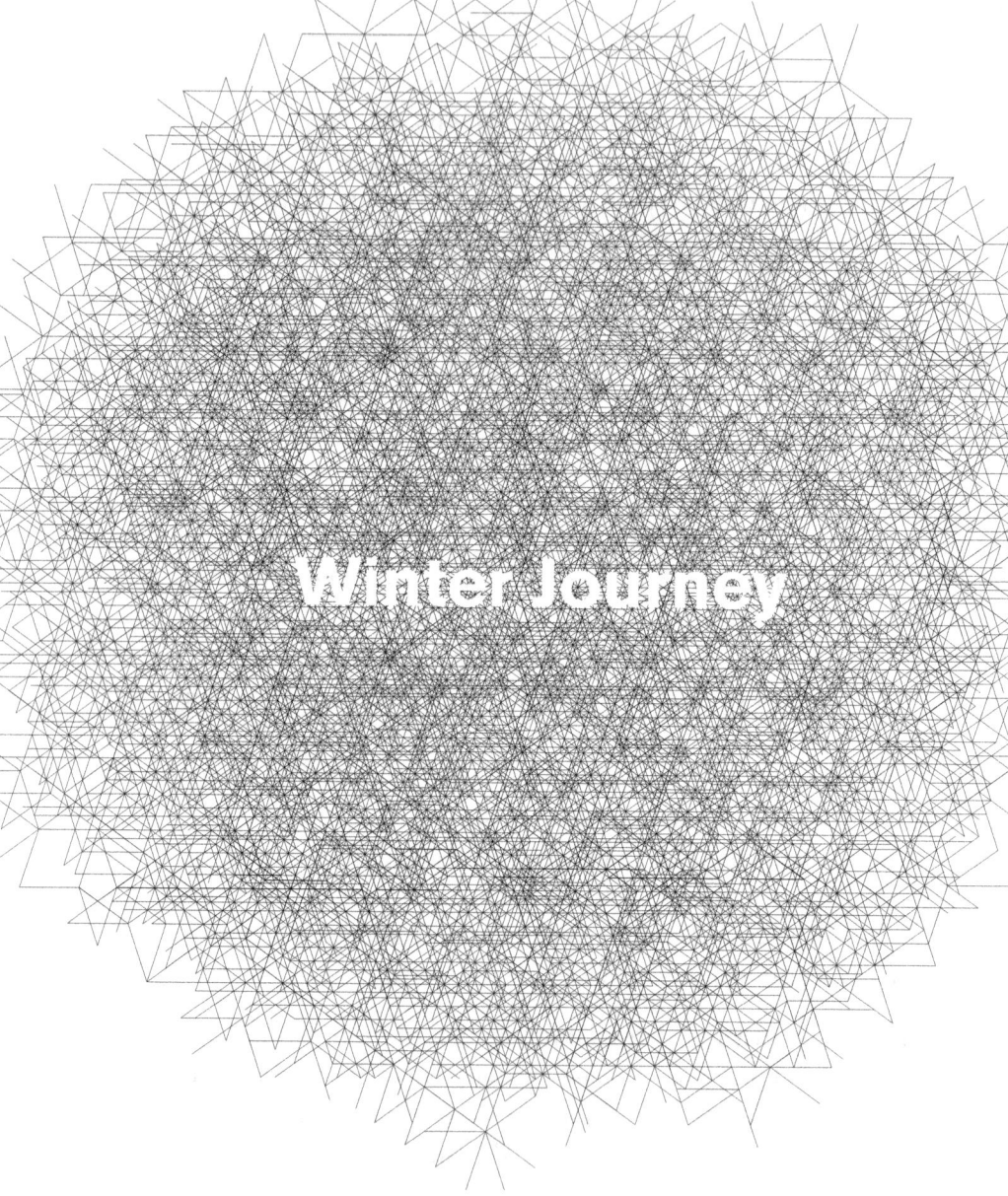

Winter Journey

Winter Morning

frost
was
broken

under the dead
leaves:

she tottered
through
the owl-howling forest,

carrying
a fox

under her numbed
arm

Rest

descending from
the snow-clad
plateau,

she
made
a halt,

the wind
died,

her cheeks
aglow
with cold

Reflection

as usual

she
looked
in the water:

the thin
ice

screened her

from
the world

below

Daylight

the cloud broke:

the trees
cast
their netlike

shadows
upon
the crusted

snow-
field

Game

she followed
faint
tracks

covered

with fresh
snow: a shot

heard,

the fox
winded

a wounded
bird

Storm

snowflakes
swirling,

crows
flew

into
the furious
sky

as if blown

by
the gale

Snowbreak

the shot
broke

the equilibrium

she
kept:

the snow
surged

into the gorge

breaking
the treacherous

ice

Bliss

hailstones
fell

filling every

depression

she left
in the snow

Winter Rain

the snow turned
to drizzle,

moistening

the dry
moss

in
the hollow
of an oak tree

thunder-
struck

Winter Sun

the glazed
ground
began to thaw:

she looked
back

to shake
the dew
from her straight hair:

the pointed
trees
stood leafless against

the slippery
sky

like
a triumph

Thaw

above
the lingering

snow

the bamboo grass
swayed
in the sun:

it blew
gently

with
the sweet scent

of mimosa

Breeze

like
a stain

of blood
a camellia
fell

on
the melting
snow

as
she passed

Magnolia

the air
shimmering

with
the heat

of the earth:

all
the buds

burst
into
white flame

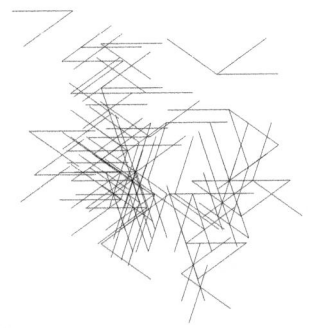

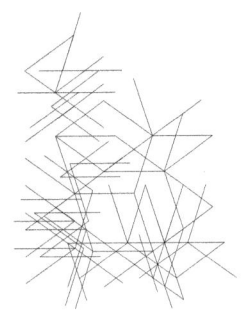

SONG OF
DESTRUCTION

one, a distant voice,

two, a waving hand,

three, a sorrowful face,

four, a drop of water,

five, an ant hill,

six, a stone,

seven, a trembling shadow,

eight, a flash of lightning,

nine, a broken bough,

ten, a pitfall,

eleven, a trodden path,

twelve, a fallen leaf,

thirteen, a tree

Scene One: A Distant Voice

all the mountains
resound
with

the shrill calls
of
birds

gathering
at
the funeral:

from
behind

the rumbling sound

of a cart
heavy
with a body, and a distant voice,

a human
cry

Scene Two: A Waving Hand

the flames
still
wavering

over
the embers

of a sprawling forest

burnt
in bloom:

the hot
air

moves

like
a huge

waving hand

Scene Three: A Sorrowful Face

the earth re-
echoes
to

the sea's roar:

after
the land-

slide

the mountain
stands

in
the
shape

of a
sorrowful

face

Scene Four: A Drop of Water

the gigantic
summits

of clouds
crumple

to a

drop
of water:

soot

falls
upon
the ruins

in heavy rain

Scene Five: An Ant Hill

the

entrances
to
an ant

hill

shrouded
by
the flow

of lava: the blind

ants

dig
their way

inward

Scene Six: A Stone

> **Through**
> **the**
> **tight**
>
> **air,**
>
> **burning**
> **and**
> **glowing,**
>
> **a stone falls**
>
> **to**
> **the**
> **earth**
>
> **at**
> **rending**
>
> **speed**

Scene Seven: A Trembling Shadow

the wind
tears

the willow's
slender branches off

its trunk:

the ruffled
lake

reflects

a trembling
shadow

of

fear

Scene Eight: A Flash of Lightning

pregnant

clouds
gather round

the sun:

the darkening
sky

is split

by
a flash
of lightning

at birth

of
a bird

Scene Nine: A Broken Bough

pine needles are
scattered
on

the wet
sand:

the whistling
grove

distorted
till

sap oozes
from

a broken
bough

Scene Ten: A Pitfall

the loosened

ground
caves
in

where runs

the subterranean
water: the oak-leaves vibrate

with
the distant

bay
of
hounds

at a
pitfall

Scene Eleven: A Trodden Path

the deep
prints

of wheels

dissolve
in the
mud:

a trodden path

fades out
in
bushes, the cradle

of
dark

eggs

Scene Twelve: A Fallen Leaf

a fallen
leaf

lost

in
an
eddy

of water:

the swollen
river

flows

into
the sea

for burial

Scene Thirteen: A Tree

under the birdless
sky

the glare

of
the
setting

sun

stains
the
bare

hillsides along
the glassy
lake:

a tree grows

from
the
scene

of
green
carnage

DANCE OF FIRE

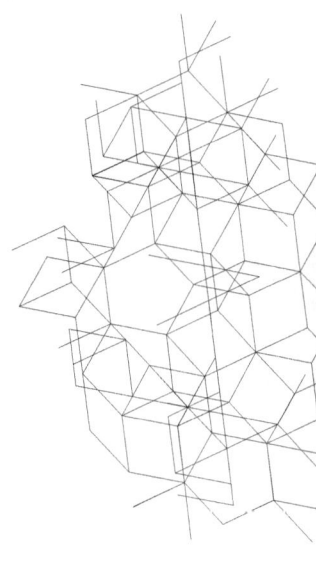

1.

passing through a needle's
eye

a wind

raised
incessant golden

waves

over
wheat fields

as if to set
on fire
the spikes

with
a forbidden

festival torch: the air

rolling
and curling upward

to a cypress'

top

2.

the wind

trampled
the soft weeping weeds

encircling

the luminous
wavering
lake:

the flaring torches
of cannas
stir

the dark

as silently
as the scarlet

silk
scarves

of barefoot dancers

3.

coming through the sunlight
above the horizon,

spreading fan-
shaped
across the grassy

hill,

frightening
a flock of still
white birds,

a field fire

ran
on tiptoe

into
the shady woods

driven
by

a fair
wind

4.

the sky aglow

as it blew
through

the blades
of pampas grass,

fanned

the smoke
of silvery flowers,

dyed

the edges
slightly carmine

as

in a
sword dance

5.

breathe in, breathe out,
fill the veins
with blood,

fill the bellows
with wind

to melt the metal
to shape
the shapeless:

the seven-colored flames
in the forge
dancing

burst into

showers
of sparks

with one blow

6.

the sun plunged
into
the sea,

a bolt of fire:

a breeze

sprang up,
a solo

after the moaning chorus
in a dumb show,

blowing out
rainbows
on the spray

of sizzling waves

7.

sea gulls

        sea swallows
            homeward

    to the light-
    house,

destroy the fire, surf-riders,

      the oil-
      smelling

      fire

    spread over the
    subdued

      sea

8.

hills
and

mountains

in smoke, the animal-
paths

barred,

the chasing
fire

swept
over

a hole

in the
withered

grassland

9.

the hydrangea
blue

deepened,

the blood
purified

in soft burning,

the
iron
wheels

rolled

over
the acid-

fruiting herbs

10.

to

a reverse
world

light coming through

a pin-
hole,

the well

ran
dry,

the
oasis

nail-
marked,

a burning wind blew up

turning the
desert

inside out

11.

deep

in
the
blue

cave

eyeless
fish

felt

the warm under
current,

rocks

burning
in the dark,

ears numb with an explosion,

sulfur

into
gas

12.

the guts
spurted

from
a volcano,

surging over valleys

and villages
at harvest time:

leaping
flames

caught

the festival
dancers

behind

severed
head

masks

13.

before its flight

feathers
rise,

eyes gleam

over its burning
territory:

lightning pierced the eagle

to the
cliff,

the nest
smashed:

rain

washed
a dusty

mirror

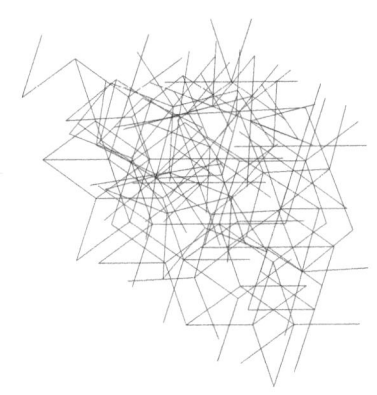

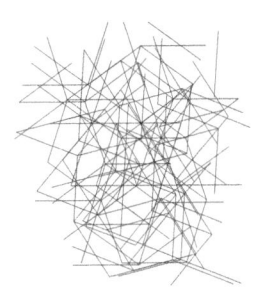

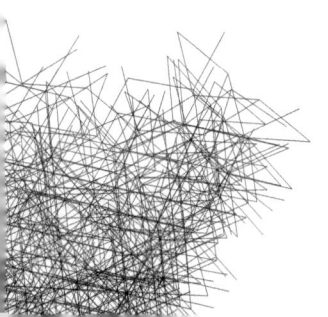

51

羽
衣

HAGOROMO
A Celestial Robe

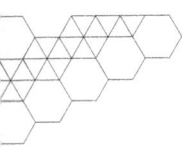

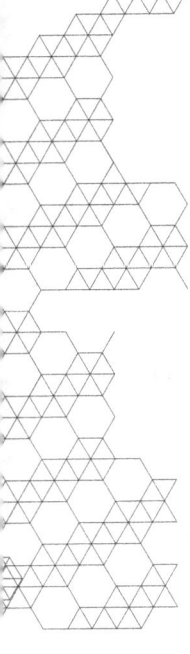

Hagoromo: A Celestial Robe

In the province of Oumi, in the south of Yogo-no-sato, there is a lake called Lake Yogo. The elders of the Yogo village have handed down a story:

A long time ago, eight celestial maidens, who transformed themselves into white birds, descended from heaven and bathed at the shore of the lake. A young man, Ikatomi, saw them at a distance from the western hill and was struck by their strange beauty. He wondered if they might be celestial beings, went down to the lake, and upon seeing them close at hand, knew that they were. Ikatomi at once fell in love and could not leave them. He secretly sent his white dog to have it steal one of the celestial robes. The dog brought back the robe of the youngest, which Ikatomi hid. The celestials became aware of their danger, and immediately the seven elder sisters flew off, but the youngest could not fly. The path to heaven was closed to her, so she stayed on the earth as a human being. (The shore, now called Kami-no-ura, Celestial Shore, is where the celestial maidens bathed.) Ikatomi married her and they lived here. She bore him two sons and two daughters. (These are the ancestors of the Ikago-no-muraji clan.) Later on, the mother found the robe and in it flew back to heaven. Ikatomi, alone on his bed, lamented.*

---

*This part is Danno's translation from a fragment of Oumi-no-kuni Fudoki, a topographical work on the Province of Oumi, compiled in the 8th century.

56

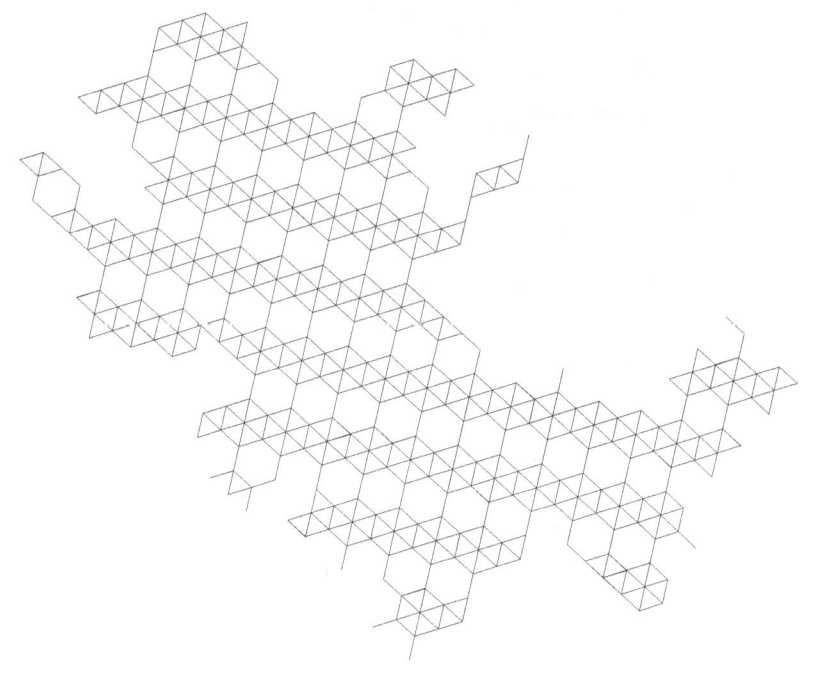

Scene One

Where am I,
standing naked in the water,
wind gently raising ripples

ruffles the willow leaves,
my long feathers,
my long hair?

Where am I,
painful in the bright sunlight,
burning green hills overwhelming me,

lake water reflecting
a young woman,
a tremor, a fear?

Where am I from?
The sudden stir in the air,
the smell of animal,

the tumult, the clamor,
the fluttering sound of wings,
and here I am,

nowhere to hide myself,
nowhere to return,
given a new body.

What am I,
this smooth soft skin,
these pliant limbs from my body?

From thirst, hands reach out
to scoop the water –
Where is my long neck, my long bill?

My white round breast,
transformed into two small mounds
aching and swelling.

This slender waist, the breathing
belly – what are you hiding,
a slit, a split?

I feel the eyes of someone
watch me, bind me
tight to the earth.

Blow, blow, blow,
O wind, shake, roll,
let fall the burning green leaves,

rip me off the trunk,
off the roots,
take me!

Scene Two

1.

Villagers, young and old,
flowers in their hair,
men and women in full bloom,

on foot, on horseback,
fishers and divers by water
from scattered islands

flock to the grassy slope,
the foot of the gods-residing
mountain bright in the morning sun.

"Today is our spring festival,
we celebrate the day,
our lord on his high seat

"praises the fertile lake
shining, surrounded,
many-folded ranges of mountains.

"Pluck up vegetables,
gather buds and blossoms for food,
inhale the fragrant fresh air."

2.

Shake, shake, shake
the golden bells in evergreen
branches, waken

the sleeping spirits, the slackening
bonfires, stamp your bare feet
on the sprouting grass,

eat and drink, sing and dance,
the full moon rising
hazy with smoke.

"My heart ruffles
like the surface of Lake Yogo
at the sight of you.

"Like waves lapping on the shore,
girls make eyes at me,
but it is you that I love.

"My heart is an island
washed by the waves of Lake Yogo,
stable and rich forever."

3.

Green leaves, hair scattered,
whirling round the tall
mulberry tree, it blows

tossing, lifting, curling to the sky,
bursting, sweeping through me,
where is it from,

where to? A boat
scudding before the wind,
a bird on the wing, an arrow shot

at tearing speed,
hoofs strike, sails fill,
the taste of sweet burning body,

smell of hills and fields
being burnt for rich
ripe fruit.

The fire unknown before
sustains me in space,
no longer to fly, nor to flee.

4.

Gently the blood is circulating
in my yielding body, or am I
floating, off the shore,

or the boat, unfastened,
down the meandering river?
Where am I from, where am I flowing?

Ame-ama, heaven and sea,
one at the horizon,
shimmer, glimmer, evaporate in blue.

Was it you who watched
me, who bound me?
Your staring eyes secure

me to land – I am sinking,
    down,
        down,
            down,

deep into the soft soil,
I am the earth, your woman,
plow me and sow seeds!

Scene Three

1.

The embers carefully kept
alive all the night –
little fires waver in the hearth

like distant memories –
of what scenes, of what world?
In the dim light come into view

the kitchen utensils –
earthen pots, pans and jars
(nuts, seeds and grain)

bottles to keep water,
pestle and mortar for brewing,
mill-stones in the nook.

Now that I have eaten food
with the people here
and drunk sake of oblivion,

what am I trying to recall?
Wake up, rekindle the dying fire,
breakfast has to be cooked.

2.

I am again in the bright sunlight
weeding the paddy-fields,
bending my back, the wind

ruffles the young rice
shooting up from the muddy water.
Here everything is visible

in broad daylight,
no secrets, no hiding, no meaning
eyes – nothing hidden

from sight, every form
revealed, breathing,
every line clean, a carved

pattern on the earthen
jar; leaves, waves, running
water; the stretch of paddy-fields,

the range of mountains, the deep
blue sky. Have I ever been up there
in my past, in my dreams?

3.

Do I see all,
do I see through all, do I
see the other side of the mountains,

or the bottom of the sky?
Do I see inside
the sealed pots in storage?

What is hidden beyond
the slit of doors
in the darkness of the cellar?

Where is the wind from,
the rain, the thunder, the lightning,
the good spirits that grow

the rice in the ear waist-high,
rustling as I pass through?
Do I see the being

growing and wriggling
in my belly, strange to feel,
yet so dear to me?

4.

Wet are my feet and the hem
of my ragged skirt,
I stand on a rock

amidst the sparkling
rapids of the clear stream –
ayu, shining, splash,

jerk my fishing threads –
I have climbed a long way
up the mountain path.

Are you, sweet fish, from afar
in your distant memory,
and accustomed to fresh water here,

placid among pebbles and plants,
dashing for shelter
from your own swift shadows?

Did you once belong to large
salt waters, or did I
to a larger world?

Scene Four

1.

Men and children out in the fields,
the head woman alone
prepares herself in the house,

cooking food with unpolluted fire,
brewing sake with pure water,
for the coming of yearly visiting spirits.

Shake, shake, shake
a thousand bells, encourage
bubbling gases, the blazing bonfire

where moths are swarming,
women, enhanced, dancing round,
green leaves in their hair,

in the fumes of summer grass,
"May no insects plague the crop,"
"May no storms thrash the rice plants,"

swirling to the empty height
where no wind ever blows,
no fire ever burns.

2.

Reeling silk off cocoons,
I see pupas, dead
before changing into moths,

tracing back in my dim memory,
a slit – a split –
and darkness beyond.

As I sit nightly
at the loom, I hear
the fluttering sound of wings,

possibly that of a hurried flight.
Why is this untiring urge
to weave a cloth

soft as down,
light as feather,
buoyant as flying spirits,

after long toil in paddy-fields,
creeping and crawling with big belly,
mowing and gleaning rice?

3.

What am I looking for
in this murky mountain, besides
oak-leaves for sake cups, basketfuls

of fruits and berries,
acorns, nuts and mushrooms?
I have gathered enough for my family

and for the coming harvest festival
when they say spirits come
to bless us from their homeland

where ancestors live forever
in light and harmony. Overhead
white birds are flying from the north,

in the woods deer belling.
I miss what I am separated from –
Not that I love you less, my beloved,

but why this urge for flight,
this yearning for the blue sky?
Earth-bound, flesh-bound, I am split!

4.

"May you descend on the holy tree,
  Touch the hallowed ground,
  Refresh our cleansed bodies,

  Life-giving spirits from over the sea,
  Bless us with abundant crop,
  Make our reed plains flourishing.

"Speak to us through the woman
  dancing airily in your robe,
  Be with us, eat with us, drink sake

  with us tonight. We offer you
  our first fruits, sing and dance for you
  to drums, flutes, koto-strings,

  the clapping of our hands. Descend
  on us all. We purified ourselves,
  our homes, our land, to receive you.

"May new life sprout from the dead,
  A new sun rise from the night,
  Shake, shake, shake

          the seeds-bearing bells."

Scene Five

1.

back
and
forth,

year
by
year,

shuttling
over
the snowfield,

along the fine warp threads,

to the arctic
zone, half-way round
the earth, on the wing in air

currents, resting on waves
at stormy night, led

by fixed
stars in mind
to the northern sky,

thread
by
thread

weaving
snow
and light

into white fabric

2.

red
green
and golden

lights,
swirling,
dancing wild,

retreat
nowhere,

the sun
stays
above the horizon

during the white summer night
of the vast thawing land,

flight feathers lost
after nuptials,

white birds
sit

on eggs
isolated

by the ice
on fire,

in this unlighted
weaving hut,

the white cloth
grows

3.

as eyes look
for words
in mind,

finger tips feel
for invisible marking
of plumage,

white
in
white,

feather in feather

intricate patterns emerging,
light-footed
dancers' steps,

in right place,
in right order,

varied,
intensified,
transformed at will,

at sunset,
at sunrise,

back and forth
between thin threads

the shuttle's
eye

gropes

4.

awakened
from dreamless
sleep

on fresh mulberry leaves
worms slough off
old skins,

growing whiter, translucent,
transformed into pupas,
in white

shelters
spun
about their bodies,

exposed
to the violent
sun's rays,

a link
of life-death cycle
breaks,

the skilled hands
spin
the filaments

of closed
cocoons
of silk moths

into dream

Scene Six

The thick, hanging clouds break,
bare of colored leaves,
trees stick out in the snow,

the lake and the mountains
covered with woven silk,
white in white, feather in feather.

Day by day I felt within
forces brewing, for a vent
gathering, increasing, threatening –

tremor – throes – strain –
down – down – down – and a push
into the flow of light and sound.

Set fire on my parturition hut,
purge the blood and stains,
a new-born life is faltering.

Out of the blue firmament
snowflakes fluttering on the flame,
smoke softly curling into the air.

Shafts of golden light
stream into the weaving hut,
the sky cleared, closed white buds

unfolding, the sealed pots
in storage opened,
at waterside, white birds,

the good spirits, bathing in the sun,
ame-tsuchi, heaven and earth,
unified, made whole.

Wave slow your scarves, my children,
keep out the evil spirits,
pacify the slain.

Drawn by the invisible threads
of light, my body floats
in windless, flameless, open space.

Where am I from, where to,
dancing in the white lucent robe,
what am I, who dreams,

                              or is dreamt?

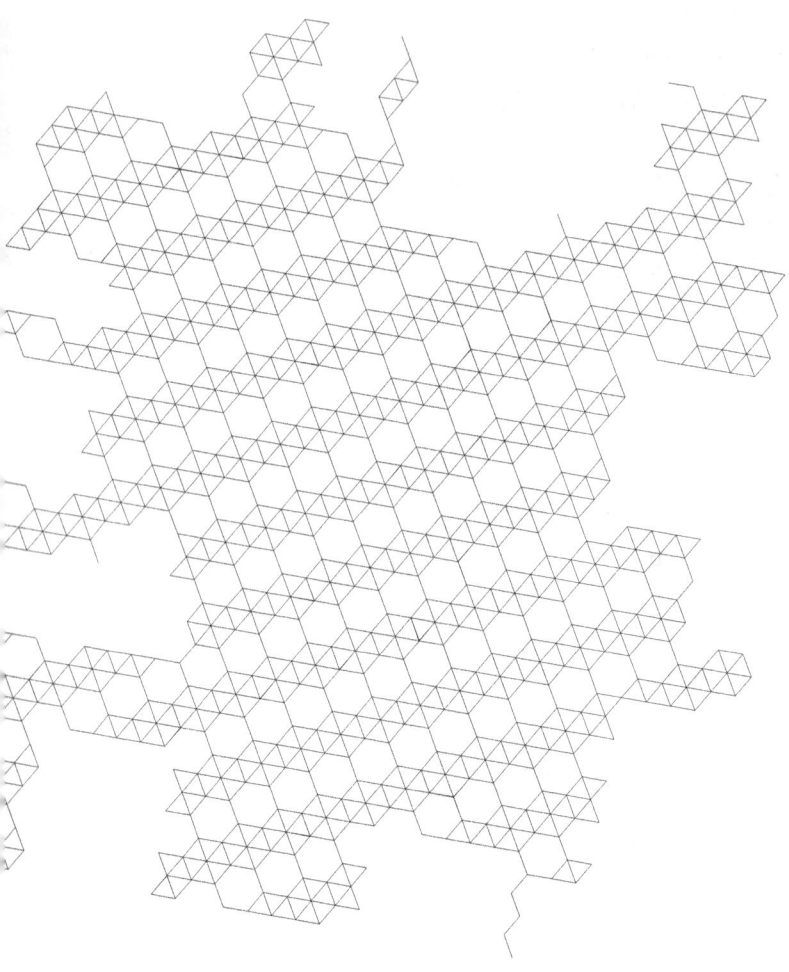

Also by Yoko Danno

Poetry:

Dusty Mirror
(with drawings by David Kidd)
The Ikuta Press, 1977

Four Songs
The Ikuta Press, 1982
(reprinted in "International Anthology of Poetry and Prose 47")
New Directions, New York, 1983

Epitaph for memories
The Bunny and the Crocodile Press, Washington, D.C., 2002

The Blue Door
(collaboration with James C. Hopkins)
The Word Works, Washington, D.C., 2006

A Sleeping Tiger Dreams of Manhattan:
simultaneous poetry, photographs and sound
(by Yoko Danno, James C. Hopkins & Bernard Stoltz)
The Ikuta Press, Kobe, 2008

Translation:

Peking Story by David Kidd
(translation into Japanese)
Sekai-bunka-sha, Japan, 1989

Songs and Stories of the Kojiki
(English version with illustrations by Horaku Nakamura)
Ahadada Books, Toronto/Tokyo, 2008

About the author:

Yoko Danno is Japanese, born, raised and educated in Kobe, Japan. A graduate of Kobe College, she writes poetry solely in English. Several books of her poems and translations have been published in Japan, the US and Canada, and her poems have also appeared in international magazines, e-journals and anthologies. Not only being a poet, she is also a translator and the editor at The Ikuta Press, a small press in Kobe.

www.ingramcontent.com/pod-product-compliance
Lightning Source LLC
Chambersburg PA
CBHW072018170626
46813CB00005B/2176